The ... ELESS Guide to... TRAVEL

By Seán Dalton, Seán Kelly, and David O'Rourke

RW Publishing

www.rwpublishing.net

First published in Ireland in 2019
by rwpublishing
An RW company

ISBN: 978-1-9993128-2-4

www.rwpublishing.net

Newsletter

Thanks for buying this book! If you enjoy reading this book, make sure to check out our newsl—

What are you doing?

I’m just trying to get you to join our newsletter. It really hel—

The book hasn’t even started yet.

So?

How can you ask me to join your newsletter when I haven’t even read the book yet? How would I know whether I like it or not? Are you an idiot?

Well, no. And no, I don’t believe I am an idiot. I was only trying to get you to keep it in mind while reading the book. You know, just in case you like it.

Then put it at the end.

What?

Put it at the end of the book. So, if I make it that far I know that I might want to sign up.

But what if people don’t read that far? Then, we won’t get any email addresses.

If people don't read that far then you don't deserve their email addresses. Why would I join your newsletter if I can't even finish the book?

Yeah but what if we don't get any email addresses?

Then write a better book!

Ayo woah aye. You haven't even read it yet.

And if you keep talking, I won't read it at all. Now put it at the end of the book.

Fine, relax.

Contents

Intro

You're on the plane to Funnyland. In the unlikely event that there should be an incident during the flight, we will now demonstrate what to do in such a situation. On your journey you may lose oxygen as a result of laughing too much. In this scenario go watch some Lee Evans. We guarantee you'll stop laughing.

This book is a compilation of some of the finest travel guides known to man. We found some incredible people who wrote some fascinating pieces on cities all around the world. From Rome to Dublin and back, we've covered the globe. We tried to keep these pieces to ourselves. Oh, how selfish we were! One night, a Saturday I believe, we took a hard look at ourselves in the mirror. What had we become? Could we really live like that? We couldn't. We just had to share it with you. We couldn't have people going their whole lives without the knowledge available in this book.

So, here we are. You might as well read it.

Rome

Location: Italy
Population: 2.8 Million
Language Spoken: Italian
Notable Inventions: Roads, Togas, and Social Welfare
Notable People: Julius Caesar, Francesco Totti, and the guys who killed Jesus

Ah Rome - Home of the Renaissance. A city most known for taking several days to build. There is more than meets the eye with this beautiful city. My name is Joshua and I am going to tell you what you *need* to do when in Rome! You're probably asking yourself, "Has this guy even been to Rome? How do I know I can trust him?" Well, of course I have been to Rome. We're talking about the capital of Italy here! Why would I lie about that? You literally have no proof that I haven't been there. I have. I've been to Rome.

Let's start with food. The food in Rome is incredible. I mean, wow. I was blown away when I visited. After arriving in Rome Airport on my first day, I travelled to my hotel in Rome City. I was so hungry after my flight, but luckily my hotel was right beside one of the most well-known restaurants in Italy. I can't remember the exact name, but it was something like Luigi's, but with a 'z'. So, I think it was Zuigi's. Although I can't remember the name, I can absolutely remember the delicious meal I ordered. I ordered what the Italians call 'a pizza pie'. Flattened dough covered in cheese, topped off with some form of sliced Italian meat! It was like there was a party in my mouth and the catering at said party was top tier. A taste of heaven. I also very cheekily had a glass of red wine with my meal. I wasn't going to, but I decided that I might as well, because as the old saying goes, "When you are in Rome." If pizza isn't your cup of tea, then I would direct you toward Italy's other famous dish: Pasta. I had the best pastas of my life while I was in Rome: Spaghetti Bolognese, Carbonaro, you name it!

…………………………………………………………………… ………………………………

Special Hint: A lesser known food to try while in Italy would be the lasagna. It is a gorgeous, cheesy dish. All I will say is if you have a cat, he might like it! That's a little joke for any Garfield fans out there. However, he would also get very sick as cat's digestive systems cannot process garlic – one of the key ingredients of the delicious meal. I always found this to be a big issue with Garfield, so I could never really immerse myself in the Garfield world. That's not to say I didn't enjoy some of the comic strips. I did. It's just that I find it hard to relate to a character when their whole personality has been set around what is essentially a falsehood and an impossibility. Unless Garfield has a different digestive system to other cats, of course. However, that has never once been suggested in any of the comic strips, and if they were to suggest it now it would feel too much like retconning for it to work as far as I'm concerned.

…………………………………………………………………… ………………………………

Food aside, what is Rome really known for? The attractions! The art, the spectacular architecture, and the history! When I was in Rome, I made it my mission to visit all of the most important pieces of Roman history: the Vatican, the Colosseum, the Sistine Chapel. I was so excited to see them that I actually saw them all in a single day! What a day might I add. My day started off with the Colosseum, which was a 5-minute walk from my hotel. I arrived there at 8am sharp! For those who are unfamiliar with the Colosseum it is essentially a football stadium, except it's where the gladiators used to fight each other in front of the crowds. So, imagine a boxing match but it's in a football stadium and the winner will get a thumbs up or a thumbs down from the President of Rome, deciding whether they live or not. And instead of boxing gloves they used, like, weapons and stuff. I assumed it would be very illegal to do this today, but you can still go to the Colosseum, so maybe it isn't. If I was to describe the Colosseum experience in one word it'd be 'huge'. It's very big.

After that I walked 20 minutes to get to the Vatican. This is where the Pope lives. I was very lucky, because I actually bumped into the Pope while I was there. He was in disguise, so I barely even recognised him. He didn't say anything to me as I walked by him, but he gave me a look – a look as if to suggest that God approves of me… a look of comfort. It was a surreal experience. It's hard to describe exactly how I felt in that moment. I remember shedding a tear as he rollerbladed away. Overall, seeing the Vatican was a great experience. The Catholic Church get a bad rep for some reason but based on what I saw they're not *that bad.* To be honest, it's probably just a bandwagon thing. I remember when I was younger, I used to hate One Direction, because that was the 'in' thing at the time. No man was allowed to like them. Every other guy my age would say, "That's gay! You can't listen to that!" but I loved every one of their songs. It took me a long time to accept that I was actually gay myself. Maybe I should go away from the bandwagons and towards groups that will accept me even if I am gay, for example, the Catholic Church.

The rest of the trip was fine. With the Sistine Chapel you get exactly what you expect. It's a church with nice pictures on the ceiling. The same must be said for Saint Peter's Basilica. Keep in mind I am colour blind, so I can't enjoy the full experience of the art. I see everything in black, white and lemon yellow. It's not easy, but there's not much I can do about it. On that same day I visited the Trevor Fountain on my way back to the hotel. It's a very nice fountain I must say. The water in it looks great and the fountain itself looks well built. Sturdy.

The only disappointing part of the holiday was that I didn't get to see the Roman army. I kept reading about it and watching videos online about how the Roman army were incredible and I had been looking forward to seeing them in person. I was hoping to maybe see them just marching the streets or practicing, but no luck. I kept asking people, “Where is the Roman army, with their pikes and their shields? Where’s this big turtle army I keep hearing about? Slow and steady didn’t win the race for them though, did it?” At first, they just laughed, thinking I was joking. I wanted to be clear that I was serious, so I kept at it; I kept asking. The more I persisted the more the laughs slowly vanished. However, the answers never appeared. I don’t know, it just seems odd to me that they would have the Vatican, home of the Pope, so close to the location of the Roman army, the people who killed Jesus. Is the Pope not mad at them? Or is this an example of extreme forgiveness? Like, maybe the Pope said not only do we forgive you guys, but we’re actually going to become your neighbours. I mean the Bible does says something about loving your neighbours. Or maybe it’s a power move by the Roman army; maybe they’re rubbing it in the Pope’s face as if to say, “What are you going to do about it, old man?” Granted, I’m not very familiar with Italian politics.

Rome was my first experience of Italy and I have no doubt that it won’t be my last. I plan on visiting Venice soon, hopefully within the next few months. If Rome was this good, then I can only imagine how good a city where everything is made of water must be. That’s all for now, however. I hope you found my guide to Rome helpful. To quote the Italians, “I bid you an Addio.”

Bangkok

Location: Thailand
Population: 8.2 Million
Language Spoken: Thai
Notable Inventions: Thai Curry, Muay Thai, Ong Bak, and Spiritual Awakenings for Wealthy College Kids
Notable People: Tony Jaa, Bam Bam, and the Guy Who Invented Thai Curry

I could feel my body being spiritually awakened as I stepped foot on the Thai soil. The air I was breathing was thousands of miles from my birthplace, yet it made me feel more at home than ever before. I originally ventured for Asia with the hopes of discovering pieces of history and a taste of their incredible culture. While this did happen, I ended up finding something far more extraordinary. I found myself.

The world is like a book, and I feel if I were not to travel the world then I would only be reading the first page. I would be missing the most significant chapters of my life. Perhaps my life before Thailand was merely the prologue and this trip is what will set my story in motion - a story of self-love, acceptance and understanding. Even as I write this now, I feel the positivity flow through my veins, as though my ancestors are telling me how proud they are of me. I can feel them around me. I want to tell them how proud I am of them, for all they did for us as a species.

The weather in Thailand was incredible. It was 86 degrees almost every day and the Sun was shining as bright as the potential of a young child's mind. This made trips to the beach essential. One afternoon, as I sat on the Thai beach, just my book of poetry and I, I could sense what can only be described as comfort. A calming feeling. I could be back home in the US, working my way up the corporate ladder, but instead I chose this. Or did this choose me? Hmm. I was doing what others would call crazy. But is it really crazy to want to live my life? – to want to delve into the extraordinary cultures of those who live on the opposite side of our beautiful planet. These other… human beings. I was challenging myself and doing what I needed to do. I suppose I had taken the road less travelled and that has made all the difference. I would ask some of the Thai people to take a photo of me on the beach. How unusual it must have been for them to see a phone with a camera, but I feel I needed to show them. Perhaps there could be a middle ground between our technological knowledge and their spirituality. Somewhere we could meet, unite, and prosper together.

I feel like despite paying for my flights and accommodation here, this trip has in fact made me richer. And I don't mean 'rich' in the monetary sense – this capitalistic system we all obey in return for materialistic rewards. No, I mean 'rich' in terms of the things that truly matter. I'm richer spiritually than ever before. My purse might not be full of dollar bills, but my mind is overflowing with ideas. I can thank Thailand for this. It's opened my eyes holistically and now I understand that I was never truly awake. The planet is dying, children are starving, and Bono from U2 isn't paying his taxes. We need to do something about it. We need to unite and heal the divide. What if we were to create a system where we exchange love and vibes instead of money? How rich we would all be… Hmm. These are just my post-meditation thoughts – the ideas stemming from my tree of enlightened perception.

Each morning I would escape to the nearby temple. This escape was more spiritual than physical, yet afterwards I felt incredible. I would spend each morning meditating for an hour, just as the monks did thousands of years ago. My mind would oscillate to the vibrations of the hums until eventually I would reach the meditation gate. Upon entry into the realm of calm, my mind began to foster new ideas and possibilities. It was at this point I knew I had to give back. I made it my mission to join a volunteer group and help those less fortunate. I didn't care that I wasn't being paid, because knowing that people's lives would be improved was payment enough.

Brick by brick we put together this new house – this home that would save the lives of many. While my friends were climbing that corporate stairs, I was piecing together this puzzle of homelessness. I was saving people's lives. It feels good to give back, especially to those less fortunate. There's such an important lesson to be learnt from observing the Asian people. They are so happy despite not being in America. That deluded sense of being is what makes them so happy and kind. Part of me wishes I was born in the slums of Asia as opposed to the suburbs of America. Oh well. Perhaps in another life.

At one stage I was lucky enough to get a photograph for Instagram with a tiger! People will tell you that they're too dangerous, because they're wild animals, but my experience with this 'wild' animal was incredible. They're not too dissimilar to humans. I could sense his comfort when I came to get the photo. He was very sleepy and relaxed, which is, like, so similar to the lazy, orange cat I had when I was younger. At the end of the day they are all just cats. thousands of years of evolution connecting them in ways too difficult for even a human mind to comprehend. These evolutionary linkages aren't just felt by animals in the same family, because I too feel very sleepy at times. What I was told was a vitamin B12 deficiency may just be an evolutionary phenomenon passed on by our cat ancestors. Hmm. Much to ponder.

My time riding an elephant was even more beautiful. Being on top of these gorgeous creatures I felt like my ancestors did. I still can't understand how poachers can kill these fragile giants in the wild. They make me sick. And the people that fund them by paying for the tusks are just as disgusting! They're part of the problem just as much as the poachers. I could never be a bystander like that. However, as I rode the Thai elephant that I paid to ride, I let these abhorrent thoughts escape me while I ventured back to the mediation gate one breath at a time.

The food in Thailand is beyond description. It made me realise how inauthentic all the food is back home. Why are we feeding ourselves these processed foods and GMOs when we could be eating like the Thai people do – the right way. The pad Thai from the local street carts were both cheap and delicious. It's the kind of food that I wish we ate back in America. Overall, the trip was like the first chapter of my new life. Going out of my comfort zone and going to the lesser travelled Thailand was the greatest decision of my life. My new-found perspective has changed my life and I look forward to using it to save the lives of many. I can't wait to tell everyone about this.

Amsterdam

Location: Netherlands
Population: 420,000
Language Spoken: Dutch and broken English
Notable Inventions: The Not-Flooding-the-Country-Machine, Clogs, and the Bike
Notable people: Ruud van Nistelrooy, Anne Frank the Tank, and Van Halen

4am on a Sunday morning, I boarded the plane and took my seat.

"We have lift off!" I said as the plane took off.

"We have touchdown!" I announced as the plane landed. With that, I myself began the applause for the short, safe journey the pilot had taken us on.

And so, my journey of 'The Dam' began! I waited at the baggage belt for my bag to turn up, but it was extremely hard to recognise it! They all seemed to look the same from my perfectly average height of 4 foot 7 inches. Eventually, my bag turned up (The one with a sticker of a plane on it). Unfortunately, I couldn't put the mountain of bags I had dragged off of the belt back on. They were too heavy, and I had urgent business to attend to.

There I stood in the middle of Amsterdam Square. The square that was more of a rectangle if I was being completely honest with myself, but I was there to enjoy myself, so I let it slide this time. There I waited for my guide, a man that goes by the nickname of Hempboy. Me standing in Amsterdam Square proved slightly problematic, as many people walking past me seemed to be waiting for a man called 'Charlie'. Many walked by me and said, "Charlie?" and I would quickly respond with, "No, no, I am Andrew." It's perfectly understandable as 4 foot 7 inches is the perfectly average height all around the world, meaning I am commonly mistaken for others from afar.

Hempboy turned up and he looked very tired. His eyes were red. The areas under his eyes were baggy too. He slurred his words and don't even get me started on his posture. However, he did seem to be in good humour regardless! Commonly I would catch him laughing to himself.

"What's first, Hempboy! Anne Frank museum? Rent out a few bikes? Shopping for bulbs in the Red-Light District?" I asked with excitement.

"Munchies," he mumbled back to me.

"Oh boy, a restaurant! I am quite peckish now that you say it!"

My tour guide brought me over the canals, where I saw paddle boats, tour boats, and even booze cruises! Such good culture. After about 30 minutes, he had brought me into a Coffee Shop. I'm more of a tea guy, but I said, "Flip it! I'm on holiday, give me all the coffee you got. No sleep for Andrew tonight!"

I told a lie. It seemed as though I would be sleeping, as he came back to my table with just a bottle of water and some cake. The cake tasted so weird. I never tasted anything like it before; the aftertaste lingered for a while and the water didn't really help. Even after the cake I still wasn't full. Hempboy was almost asleep beside me, so I tugged on his jacket and asked if it would be ok if I had more cake but just in a different flavour. He just nodded, put his hood up, and went back to sleep. I wandered up to the shopkeeper and asked what other cakes she had. She showed me a range of different cakes; I spied brownies at the corner of my eye.

"Brownies! Andrew loves brownies!" I cheered. "Andrew is hungry! Can I have 5 of those brownies? And quickly! Andrew's HUNGRY!"

I ate the brownies quicker than you could say, "I AM AMSTERDAM." They filled my tummy up all nice and warm, but the taste of the brownies was only slightly better than the cake, which was disappointing. Hempboy woke up in a daze and asked what I wanted to do. I suggested the Anne Frank house. We hopped on two bikes and were on our way!

My god was that a long cycle; 'sweaty' wouldn't even begin to describe it. When we parked our bikes, I started to feel lightheaded, but was determined to push on to the house. We headed inside with a group of tourists. It was so emotional. How could they go through that? I was slowly realizing the similarities between Hitler and the big bad orange man in America. It SCARED me! The most unusual thing happened when we climbed into the attic. Everyone else seemed calm but I began hyperventilating, losing feeling in my toes and what I saw was a bit out of the ordinary.

"Does nobody else see those 50 rats sitting in the corner staring at me!?" I asked with shivering panic in my voice.

Everyone shrugged, shared concerned glances and continued about their own business.

"HAHAHA, yeah I was only joking!" I said in an attempt to ignore the rats like the others were. I don't know what it was about that house, but strange things continued to happen. Without boring you with the details of it, I could feel a giant wart growing at a rapid pace in my stomach, but I was too afraid to tell anyone at the time.

Next, once I was done telling those rats to stop following me, Hempboy brought me to the Van Gogh museum to check out all of his famous art. It would have been something to tick off of my bucket list. Regrettably, Hempboy may have gotten some bad information. The place he brought me wasn't a museum at all, but a house of mirrors with a huge pit in the middle. I hugged the wall to avoid the pit as best as I could. We weren't in the 'museum' for too long until we were forced out by security.

"You rip painting! You rip painting!" shouted Hempboy.

"Yes, I am Andrew," I said, struggling to understand his broken English.

Amsterdam was full of surprises. For example, I didn't realise it had such a huge rat problem. Remember the 50 I told to leave me alone? Well there were now at least 1,000 waiting for me outside the 'museum'. Hempboy acted as if this was normal. Very bad culture in my opinion.

Overall, I don't think I would go back. I felt so tired after one day of being a tourist in Amsterdam that I stayed in bed for the rest of the next day. It was just as well I did, because I hate Mondays.

Las Vegas

Location: United States
Population: 0.64 Million
Language Spoken: American
Notable Inventions: Sex, Drugs, and Rock and Roll
Notable People: Frank Sinatra, David Copperfield, The Blue Man, and The Other Blue Men

VEGAS, BABY! The city of sin! Me and THE BOYS went to Vegas about three weeks ago. Picture this: a group of four problematic bachelors roaming around the city of sin, scarves left at home. Talk about a wild time! It was just me *(Mr. Trouble)*, Peter *(Hard Man Jones)*, Tommy *(Cynical Clive)*, Josh *(The Wildcard)*, and a weekend of possibilities. We painted the city red and did all there is to do when in Vegas. Today I'm going to share with you what you should do when in Vegas based on my experience.

Before we got there, we agreed that we would go straight to the casino. The plan was to bet 20,000 dollars each on red in the roulette. The idea was that if we win, we were going to have the craziest fricking holiday ever. If we lost, we were going straight home. The kind of stuff only a bunch of crazy dudes could think of. We told the taximan to bring us straight to the MGM Grand. He told us we were bad men. We told him he's dead right. We walked in there with shenanigans written all over our demeanour and placed our money on red. "Call us the Crimson Crew," I told the dealer. He did not. And then, unfortunately, it landed on green. We couldn't hide our disappointment. Tommy started saying, "I knew this would happen." Then, suddenly, Josh started laughing.

"Hey guys," he said. "I actually put my money on green!" Classic wildcard behaviour! This is exactly what you should expect when you go on holidays with Josh. And he wasn't lying; we could see his chips on green right in front of us. In hindsight it's actually kind of weird that none of us saw him put the chips down, because we were right there. We were looking right at it.

But anyway, he won 360,000 dollars! Not a bad way to start a boy's holiday, am I right?

After that, we headed for our hotel. We were staying at the Bellagio – or should I say the BellagiUhOhHereComeTheBigMen. Josh paid for us to get the penthouse suite with his winnings. It was, like Borat would say, "Very nice!" We unpacked, showed each other our planned dance moves, and left for the lobby. We decided to go to that restaurant where they let fat people eat free. Tommy, being 400 pounds, got to eat for free. You can probably understand why he's so miserable and cynical now. It's because of his obesity. We also call him 'The Beast' because of this. Unfortunately, me and the other boys are always in tiptop shape, so no free food for us. We all had burgers and Tommy ate the equivalent of an all you can eat buffet. Afterwards he wasn't feeling the best, so he headed back to the hotel room. The rest of us needed a plan of action.

"Let's go to the slot machines!" I said.

"Nah, bro. Let's go to the slut machines! Ahhh ha ha ahh!" said Josh. We all shouted at him for saying that. I couldn't believe it. We hate that he chose to talk down on women like that. That's what you get when you bring a wildcard with you. High moments and low moments. You never know what he's going to say or do. We sat him down and explained that calling women 'sluts' is horrible and degrading. We gave him a brief history of the oppression of women and afterwards he said, "Woah… I didn't know about that. I apologise." I could tell he said that from his heart. It was definitely a turning point. After our intense discussion about how we, as men, need to start treating women as equals and with far more respect, we realised we needed to relax. So, we decided to go to the strip club. Josh even bought us all lap dances. *This* was definitely one of the high moments.

Leading up to this holiday I watched the film "21" 15 times. That's 315! I did this partially because I wanted to learn how to count cards for blackjack, but also to show solidarity for my man Kevin Spacey. He didn't do it! Are you telling me Spaceman did the things they claim he did? How could someone who is that good of an actor do all of that? And how could he have gotten away with it for so long? He hardly pretended to be normal for all those years. This isn't a film. Nobody is *that good* of an actor. Well, maybe Kevin Spacey is, but that doesn't mean he did it. What would be the odds of that! But anyway, I was looking forward to playing a bit of the old blackery jackery. I headed for the gambling floor and sat at one of the tables. "Hit me!" I said to the dealer. He told me I would need to convert my money into chips and come back. I said, "Mr. Dealer you have yourself a deal!" and went off to convert. I came back and put my chips on the deck. I told him to hit me and he told me to place a bet. I put down two big ones and told him to try his best. Then, I received my cards. It was time to start counting. I got a 10 of hearts and a 6 of spades. 10 + 6 = 16. I had 16. The aim was to get to 21. 21 - 16 = 5. That means I needed 5 more. My odds of getting 5 were 5/10. That's 50%. I like those odds! I told the dealer to hit me. I got a 4 of clubs. 10 + 6 + 4 = 20. 21 – 20 = 1. I was 1 off. *Very nice!* I stuck. He revealed his cards. A 10 and a 9. He took another. A jack. Winner winner chicken dinner. It was that easy. I continued to count cards for another hour and, as I suspected, the cards were rigged. I won about 500 dollars and lost about 1000. 1000 – 500 = 500. That means I lost 500 dollars. Not great. Not bad.

After that mild success, myself and Peter decided to hit up the poker table. Texas hold 'em. Yeehaw baby. We had a tactic. You *need* a tactic. We would wink at each other every time we had a good hand, letting the other person know that we had a good hand. This is crucial when trying to win a game of poker. It was just us, some Texan with a moustache, and a lady named Denise. Well, we rolled those cards and made a silly billy of the dealer. We were up 10 thousand dollars each. The Texan was up at least 20 thousand and Denise had raked in almost 600 thousand dollars. About an hour in the Texan looked at us and Denise and said, "Y'all wanna spruce this Bruce up a little bit?"

"How so," I inquired.

"Hows about we go all in. Every one of us. Every chip on the table." He looked to Denise. "That includes you, little missy. I wanna see all your winnins' in the middle like a fiddle."

"Well, howdy doo, I do love me a risk," she said in a put-on Texas accent. It wasn't a very good accent. Clearly not her speciality.

Well, like the pack of wild geese we were, we went all in. It was a close round, but the Texan won. After that round the dealer started waving and announcing, "The table's closed" in the accent that the train guy says, "ALL ABOARD!" in that film. You know the film I'm talking about. I looked to the dealer and asked was he that guy. He said no, but that he was in fact mimicking that guy's voice. I told him that he did an excellent job. As we left the table, the Texan called us over. To our utter shock he took off his moustache. It turns out it was Josh the whole time! He shook the 600k plus worth of chips in the air and said, "We did it again, baby! Viva Las Vegas!" Peter and I started chanting, "WILDCARD! WILDCARD!" as we threw him over our shoulders.

"We robbed that slu-" He stopped. "We robbed that lady!"

"That's more like it," I said with a wink.

We danced and skipped out way back to our hotel room, without a care in the world. When we got back to the hotel room, we found Tommy lying down on the bed. He wasn't moving. I went up to his body. He wasn't breathing. The autopsy told us that he had eaten too much at the restaurant, leading to his already high cholesterol shooting through the roof, resulting in a heart attack. We were distraught and heartbroken. We had just lost one of our good friends. We were disgusted that we had ignored the symptoms of his severe obesity. As it turns out, it wasn't beauty that killed The Beast… it was unchecked and ignored obesity. The saying goes, "What happens in Vegas, happens in Vegas." I always found this to be a bit of a redundant statement. However, after spending the weekend there I do think it works as a tagline for the city, because at the end of the day it's true. Everything that happened while we were in Vegas, happened in Vegas. It's definitely accurate. However, the scars left from this trip will mark our minds and our hearts for an eternity.

Dublin

Location: Ireland
Population: 0.5 Million
Language Spoken: Irish
Notable Inventions: The Potato, Guinness, and Depression
Notable People: Oscar Wilde, Bono, Conor Jobs, and Conan O'Brien

I recall being met by the man as I reached the arrivals floor in Terminal 1 of Dublin Airport. He told me his name was William and that he was chosen to show me around the city of Dublin. He wore a black top hat on his head and carried a cane. He was as quintessentially British as one could imagine.

"Charlie!" cried the man. "My dear boy, good to see you. My name is William and I have been chosen to show you around Dublin for your all-inclusive tour of Ireland."

"Hello, William! What are the plans for the day?" I asked.

"Charlie, our day will begin with Dublin's Trinity College. I'll show you around. Then, we'll visit the Guinness Storehouse. After that we'll end the day with a surprise before you head back to the airport."

Straight away we went to Ireland's number one University, Trinity College Dublin. It was crowded with tourists and egotistical students wearing scarves and hats and the likes. I was blown away. I remember saying, "This architecture is incredible."

William replied with, "Yes, indeed. British built."

"See this bell tower here?" he asked. He was pointing at a bell tower that stood in the centre of the campus' main square.

"That one there?" I asked, pointing at what was the only bell tower I could see. I wanted to ensure that my eyesight wasn't failing me.

"Yes. That one there." He sighed and rolled his eyes. "If a student were to try and climb it then the head of the university could legally shoot them with a crossbow."

"Oh wow. That's crazy."

"Indeed. If only the Irish knew how to climb!"

"Is that not a bit racist? And also, a bit weak of an insult?"

"No, it's a jolly good insult. And, no, the Irish are not a race. They are nothing. Anyway," he said, "let us go look at the cricket and rugby pitches, where the Irish try to play British sports!"

He continued to tell me stories and facts about the university. He told me how despite being Ireland's number one university, it wouldn't even be in the United Kingdom's top 10 universities. He then went on to laugh and mumble under his breath, "I'm surprised they even have third level institutions here."

After that we left for the Guinness Storehouse. We were to meet the taxi man on the quays of Dublin. I remember hearing chanting and marching from afar. As the noise got louder, I could begin to see people marching.

"Who are those orange men?" I asked William as I pointed toward a group of men marching over the bridge.

"You mean them?" he asked as he pointed toward the people I was pointing at.

"Yes. Surely they aren't real people."

"My dear boy, they are real people," William answered. "They're the Goomba Roombas."

"The Goomba Roombas?" I asked.

"Yes Charlie. We imported them direct from Northern Ireland!" said William proudly.

"There's no such place," I said.

"Excuse me, dear boy, but…"

"With all respect, William," I cried. "It's not a real place in and of itself!"

The orange men began chanting, "Goomba Roomba Rumpity Do. We've got a sectarian chant for you!"

Dublin city! Dublin city!
Oh, the Irish we do pity!
Potato licking no good Paddy!
As useless as an armless caddy!

When will they forget about!
The vulgar coming from their mouth!
Tá mé this and tá me that!
Shut your mouth, you Irish twat!
Get those 26 counties and ring them!
Tell them they're in the United Kingdom!

William began to clap as they marched past us.

"Adorable, isn't it, Charlie? They believe they can be British despite holding Irish blood. A fascinating bunch nonetheless."

I nodded as the tour continued. The taximan greeted us with a smile and drove us to the Guinness Storehouse. I had heard that the Guinness Storehouse is always full of tourists, but it was empty when we arrived. He must have booked the place out, as it was just him and I there.

"Charlie, you don't mind if I do the tour slightly differently today, do you?"

"Of course not!" I said.

"Great," he said. "I will share some facts with you about Guinness and Ireland, but then I must leave momentarily. I trust this will not be an issue?"

"Of course not!" I said,

"Excellent. The founder of Guinness was Arthur Guinness. He was a Protestant. Were you aware of that? Did you know that, in the 1920s, the Guinness family were the 2nd richest family in all of the United Kingdom? Can you imagine that? A group of Irishmen with all that money. An amusing thought indeed."

He brought me into the next room – a room filled with Guinness pouring from a waterfall into a river.

"This room isn't finalised yet, Charlie. We should head for the next room." He then took me to a large room. On the door it said, "Invention room: KEEP OUT!" William took a step back before kicking the door down. "That's how we do it," he mumbled to himself. The room was mostly empty, but there stood a small table in the centre of the room.

"This," William said, "is the everlasting hop. It's absolutely new. It's an experiment, but it is believed that when someone drinks with it, they will become intoxicated for incredibly long periods of time. You just put this hop into a cup of water and the water will turn to beer and the hop will never get smaller and never run out. You can keep drinking the beer by just putting more water into the cup!" His phone began to ring. "Pardon me, Charlie. I must leave you for a moment now." With that, he left the room.

I remember thinking how awful of a business idea that was for Guinness. If it truly worked then they'd soon be out of business. Why would they do that? I couldn't wrap my head around it. Anyway, it was a temptation to say the least – and a must to say the most. I couldn't resist. I grabbed the empty glass from beside it on the table. I then poured the water that was also there into the cup. After popping the hop into the glass, I remember saying, "God I hope this works." I can't remember what relevance that had to the situation, but it's what I said in the moment. Straight away I felt the buzz. It was the buzz you get after drinking 5 pints of Guinness and I was feeling it after only one sip. Crazy. I took another sip and at that stage I was on wheels; I was bagged and tagged and rolling up the walls. I can't tell if I was just ridiculously drunk or if the Goomba Roombas actually showed up again, but in my mind they did. The voices, one thousand of them singing together, came loud and clear into the room and met my ears:

Roomba Goomba Goombity Pop!
Charlie has used the everlasting hop!
Dear boy, can we at least agree?
That there is nothing worse to see!
Than when the young man drinks the beers!
We haven't seen such audacity in years!
We won't take this nonsense lazily!
For we all worship Ian P—

"OI!" William came strolling back into the room. "Get out of here you damned Goomba Roombas. I've had enough of your shouting. To be frank, I've had enough of your everything."

The Goomba Roombas scurried away as William closed the door behind them. He turned back around to me and asked, "Did you enjoy your time in Dublin, Charlie?"

"Why, yes I did, sir!" I said as I stumbled on the spot. "Are you not mad at me for using the hop?"

"Of course I'm not mad, my boy. That was the test! And I'm delighted to hear that you enjoyed your time here," said William, tapping his cane on the ground. He was now staring at me. "Yes," he said, "This is excellent to hear you say that." He began twirling his cane and performing some sort of tap dance. "Don't you see, my dear boy? Hasn't it been clear from the beginning? This whole country is now yours. I'm giving it to you!"

I didn't know what to say. I just stared at him. Eventually I built up the sense.

"Giving it to me?" I gasped. "You must be joking."

"No, my child. I'm William. And it's all yours! The fields, the roads, the Micks. They're all yours now!"

"But why?" I asked with a burp.

"Well, you see, my boy," William started, "What use would we have of them?"

....

"And that was it, your Honour. That's why I am the rightful owner of Ireland now."

The judge of the European Court of Justice stood up.

"An interesting story, Charlie," he said. "And you believe this exonerates you of the mass genocide you carried out in Longford, Ireland."

"I do, your Honour."

"And this man… William," the judge started. "This wasn't Prince William of the United Kingdom by any chance?"

"Now that you mention it, your Honour, it was. It was Prince William."

"And you understand that Prince William has no jurisdiction in Ireland?"

"No, your Honour. I was unaware of this."

"Well that seems to be the miscommunication here."

"Oh. So, he didn't actually give me Ireland?"

"No. He had no right to. He doesn't even own the Guinness Storehouse," said the judge.

"Ah. Right. I think I understand my crimes now."

"Well Charlie… The ownership of Ireland really doesn't come into the debate here. It's the genocide that we're reprimanding you for."

"Wait, so that would have been illegal even if I owned Ireland?"

"Yes."

"Okay. Then, yes, I plead guilty, your Honour."

New York

Location: USA
Population: 19.5 Million
Language Spoken: American
Notable Inventions: Coffee, Money, and The Handlebar Moustache
Notable People: 50 Cents, Spider Guy, Jon Arbuckle, and Orange Man

New York, New York! The place so nice, you say it twice. 'The Big Apple' as some people call it. What many people don't know is it got this name because of the massive 25km diameter apple buried beneath the heart of the city. The apple was placed there after the destruction of Old York by the evil giant, Dr. Doomsday. As the old adage goes, "The Big Apple today keeps the Big Doctor away."

The apple isn't the only enormous thing in NYC. As the plane arrived, I looked out the window to see the majestic Empire State Building. It was just about the tallest thing I could imagine, until I saw Long Island. The island seemed to be like any other part of the city except that everyone and everything was much longer. One man was so long that he stretched himself right up to my plane window and knocked on the glass. That was until a monkey that was just as big came along and knocked his lights out. That same monkey then picked up an innocent woman off of the street and climbed up the Empire State Building. All of this happened before my plane even landed. An interesting start to say the least.

I left the airport bright-eyed and eager to see what this beautiful city had to offer. All around me were skyscrapers so big that they must've had at least 10 floors. *Each!* What could they possibly need all those floors for? I made my way to Wall Street after reading online that the buildings there were full of bulls and bears fighting each other. To my immediate disappointment however, it was just a lot of people in suits running around with papers falling out of their briefcases shouting, "BUY LOW!" or

"SELL HIGH!" along with the occasional "HEY OH I'M WALKIN' 'ERE!"

My next stop was the famed statue of Liberia. I got into a cab and said, "Take me to the big statue, please, sir, Mr. Taximan."

"You talkin' to me?" he asked, despite the fact there was nobody else in the cab.

"Yes."

"Well I'm the only one here. Who the hell else are you talking to?"

"I am talking to you, yes."

He then explained to me that the statue was out at sea and that I'd have to take a boat to get to it.

"Well by golly, mister," I says to him, "I really wanna see that darn statue! Do you know where I can find me a mighty fine little boat?"

He responded with something along the lines of "Ay oh that's not my f****** problem you stupid motherf*****!" The people in this city seemed to scream and swear a lot of the time, which I was absolutely fine with. I didn't cry after talking to the taxi driver. Not even once.

I hopped out of the cab and paid the driver 10 bucks after moving a total of 20 feet in the midday traffic. The traffic seemed to be constant in New York, with people constantly walking in front of cars and shouting at each other. I discovered that it was a tough place where only the strongest survived. I decided to buy a snapback style hat so that I would look super tough and people wouldn't mess with me. I found one that quite simply said "I (heart) NY." I presumed there must have been a Neil Young concert around that time. I put the hat on and looked in the mirror. *Something's not right…* I thought to myself, before I was struck with inspiration. I took the hat off, turned it backwards so it was facing the opposite direction and then placed it on my head. When I walked out of the store, I could see people running away from me in fear. A crackhead woman who was about to mug me saw my hat and then gave me all her money instead. An African

American man told me that I looked "Tight." I was feeling confident and cool as all heck. I was finally starting to fit in.

As I walked by a local sandwich shop, I saw a greasy looking fellow wearing a wife beater, tracksuit pants and a gold chain. He was clearly shouting at and intimidating the owner. I walked in with my hat on securely and shouted, "Hey! What's going on here?" The man turned around with a surprised look on his face. He took his cigar out of his mouth and waved it around as he said "Ayy this kid's got a lot o' balls," to absolutely nobody. He picked up a crowbar that was lying next to him and smacked me across the head. I was unconscious instantly.

When I woke up, I was in a dark room filled with cigar smoke. I was sitting in a chair. A man with greased up hair in a fancy suit was sitting in front of me

"Ohhh, he's awake now," said the cigar man in the corner of the room. "Some set of balls on this guy, boss."

"Yea, this kid's got a real pair o' nuts," said a shockingly similar looking man on the other side of the room.

"Do you have any idea who I am, kid? Eh?" said the bossman in a thick Italian accent. I shook my head. "I'm Vito Spaggalione. I'm the leader of this here crew. We seem to have a little misunderstanding, you and me. You insulted one of my men, big Paulie FatLips over here, and you understand, I cannot allow this. I've gotta save face, you know what I'm sayin', kid? Now, I'll admit, you got a real pair o' stones-"

"Yeah, boss, a fat sack o' balls, no question."

"HUGE cajones."

"-and I like that, kid, I do, but you know how it is. Paulie, get me that big knife over th-"

"AY PAULIE!" shouted a fourth man from behind me.

"YEA, WHAT'S YOUR FUCKIN' PROBLEM?"

"I ASKED FOR FUCKIN' SALAMI, YOU FAT GAVONE."

"OHHHHHHH," the men in the room all cried in unison.

"YOU WANNA FIGHT ME COCKSUCKER, EH?"

"AYYYY OHHHH. FUCK YOUR MOTHER, YOU PAZZO."

"OHHHHHHHHHHH," the men once again screamed aloud.

All the men in the room then engaged in an intense shouting match with a lot of over-the-top hand gestures and crazy facial expressions. In the commotion I was able to quite effortlessly get up and walk out of the room. Right as I left, I heard as their altercation came to an end, and they all started embracing each other saying, "Fuhgetaboudit" to one another. They didn't seem to even notice I was gone.

I found myself humbled by the whole experience, so I decided to just lay low and see the rest of the touristy sites while I still could. I made my way to the top of the Empire State Building, where I was greeted by a man who claimed to be the Emperor of New York himself.

"So, you see, if you just give me 48 seconds," he eagerly said to me, "I can explain to you how to make millions. You see this city? It's my city. I love to ride around New York in my helicopter. This could be you someday. If you just buy my book '*How To Become Really Really Rich Without Having To Do Any Work At All (I Swear It's Legit)*' you can make all this money no problem. I know what you're thinking. Too good to be true, right? Well...". He carried on like this for what I can only imagine was far longer than 48 seconds. Would the emperor really lie? He followed me in the elevator back down to the ground floor which I can assure you took closer to 48 minutes. I managed to get rid of the man after a lot of running.

After dining on the local cuisine of pretzels and pizza greasier than Paulie FatLips' hair, I decided to take an evening stroll around my neighbourhood. After being stabbed for the third time on my way to Central Park, I realised this was not a good idea and decided to wait until the following morning to leave my hotel again. At the crack of dawn, I made my way into the city. I started the day with a nice cup of coffee and a bacon sandwich in "Central Pork." I had only just sat down when I was greeted by a worried looking man with a long face. He came right up to my table and asked, “Have you seen Rachel?!” with sweat dripping from his forehead. I responded by telling him that I had no idea who that is. His eyes widened and he pulled what had to be the goofiest face I have ever seen. He held this face for several seconds, as though waiting for the people around him to stop laughing before shouting, “RAAAACHELLLLL!” in a guttural scream. He tried to leave the shop but ran straight into the glass door and fell backwards onto the floor. “Well, that’s not good!” he announced and pulled the same goofy face. *What an absolute character*, I thought to myself. *I would just love to see more of his wacky adventures.*

That was just about it for my journey to the wonderful land of NYC. Ultimately, I found it to be an absolutely terrifying place, and I would love nothing more than to never go anywhere near it again. Even just thinking about it sometimes gives me panic attacks and severe anxiety. I haven’t properly slept since I’ve come home, and I probably never will again. Overall, four stars.

Toyko

Location: Japan
Population: 9.2 Million
Language Spoken: Japanese
Notable Inventions: The Nintendo, Robots, and Anime
Notable People: Hideo Kojima, Yoko Ono, and Steve Aoki

My trip to Toyko, Japan was otherworldly. At the time I had never left Europe, so this holiday was truly a step out of my comfort zone. My friend, Paulie, came with me and we explored the wonders that Japan had to offer. The differences from home were insane… mind-blowing. The entire trip was unbelievable. Yet, it did happen. I did go to Toyko. And now I'm going to share with you what the beautiful city is like.

When we think of Toyko we all usually think of robots, gadgets, and gizmos. Yet, even knowing this, I was still shocked by how prevalent they were. They were everywhere. Once you land in the airport, you're escorted off the plane and into the Toyko Airport by what they call the 'AARGH' – or the Airport Assistance Robot Greeting Helper. It's translated from Japanese, so the acronym isn't entirely accurate in terms of English grammar. AARGH walked us through passport control and into the baggage claim area. From there another robot took over. This particular robot helped us collect our bags. His name was Baggage Robot Unloading Helper, or 'BRUH'.

Toyko is known as being one of the safer cities in the world to walk around as a traveller. I was unsure as to why this was the case, but the reason becomes very clear once you're there: they have Police Drones and Robocops patrolling the whole city. It's surreal, but you definitely feel safe. We actually witnessed one incident where a man grabbed a bag from an elderly lady and tried to run away. The man was immediately caught by two of the Robocops, like, literally within seconds. We were very impressed. We overheard them say they were bringing him to a place called Unit 732, which I assume is the name of their police station or their court of law. Knowing the Japanese, their prisons are probably like staying at a hotel anyway!

Japan are also very well known for their games. Whether it be Nintendo or Sony, the Japanese know how to make a game console. They also know how to make revolutionary arcade games. We went to this arcade place I was recommended to go to called Land of Doom. It was incredible. I couldn't believe that some of these games were actually real. Of course, we were helped around by one of their helper robots - Game Assistance Robot (For Individuals Entering Land of Doom), or GARFIELD. They were clearly familiar with the comic strips as they programmed him to say such things as, "The Mondays! AHHH. They displease me very much!" and "Let us get the lasagna. I lust for it." I wasn't crazy about it if I'm being honest. If anything, it took away from the experience. It wasn't necessarily what the robot was saying that was bothering me, it was more the frequency of his comments. It was non-stop.

Aside from the robot cat, the Land of Doom was great. We played games that I didn't even know existed: *Call of Duty: Samurai Warfare, Tony Hawk's Mid-Life Crisis*, and *Donkey Kong & Geralt of Rivia at the Special Olympics Games*. My personal favourite was the Toyko version of *Tetris*. The game is kind of similar to the Western version, but the music was slightly more oriental. I even beat Paulie in a game of *Dance Dance: Yeet Street*, which was disappointingly the exact same as *Dance Dance: Revolution*. They even had games made specifically for the elderly – games that were crafted to help maintain an elderly person's cognitive ability and improve their memory. These games included *Brain Training, Mario Kart: Meals on Wheels*, and *Sudoku in VR*. Overall, I probably spent nearly 50 Euro worth of Yen in there. Needless to say, it was good value for a great time.

Paulie had just turned 34 the day we arrived, so that night we decided to go to a bar. While he was in the bathroom, I snuck off and asked the barman if we could surprise him with a cake. The barman bowed. Once Paulie came back, we reminisced about old times and people we had forgotten. A few hours had passed and there was no cake in sight. Had the barman misheard me? Just as I was about to go up and ask again, the music changed. This wouldn't usually catch my attention, but it was a very abrupt change. Suddenly there was 80s style music echoing around the bar. It was really weird. Not my cup of tea. Next thing we know the room starts filling up with 80s style robot servants. *'Oh no. We came to the wrong bar!'* I remember thinking. I thought we were about to get into a kerfuffle with some old-school, ass-kicking robots. Suddenly, they all started to throw themselves towards us. As I adjusted myself into my Karate stance, they all started screaming, "HAPPY BIRTHDAY, PAULIE!" I must have asked for a birthday robot and not a birthday cake. To be fair I was pretty tipsy, and I have a habit of slurring my words once the drinks start flowing. Paulie quite liked it, though, so it wasn't all bad. It was a simple miscommunication. It was a surprise, to be sure. But a welcome one at that.

On our final day we encountered the weirdest thing I have ever experienced in all my years of travelling. I can handle robots and well, more robots, but this thing caught me off guard. I don't understand why it even exists. It shook me to my core. We were shown what the Japanese refer to as 'Anime'. It was like a cartoon, but it seemed to be purposely drawn poorly. It had a story, but the story seemed to be purposely over the top and dramatic. Everything about it scared me. The worst part was that our hotel for the final night was called the 'Anime Hotel'. We didn't realise what that meant when we booked it. Everybody working there was in cartoon form and most seemed to be 15-year-old girls. I didn't even think it was legal to employ children. What's worse is that there weren't even any robots. It's like the only hotel in all of Toyko that doesn't have robots. This was such a pity, because the robots had really grown on me at that stage of the holiday.

Earlier in trip we had been invited to a house party in the centre of Toyko that happened to be on our final night. We didn't want to sit around and watch Anime all day, so we decided to hit up this party and kick back with some punch. But first, we went to a restaurant to line our stomachs before a big night of drinking. We went to a place called Shiba Shiba Kai – a quant restaurant down a mysterious alleyway in centre Toyko. The rain was pouring down from above the 10 story tall buildings enclosing the alleyway. It was here where we discovered the Japanese dish of sushi. It was the only option on the menu, so I asked the waiter, "Pardon me, good sir, but what exactly is sushi?" He told me that it was essentially fish and rice. "I've heard of fish and chips," I said, "but fish and rice? Now you have my attention! I'll have one, please." Paulie ordered the same, mainly because it was the only thing on the menu. After we finished the meal Paulie remarked, "Fish and rice? I've heard of fish and chips, but this?" I asked him did he not hear me say that to the waiter literally ten minutes previous. He said he didn't because he was on his phone. I'm inclined to believe him as well because it would be odd to repeat it if he already heard me say it. Also, he was on his phone at that time. I suppose great minds think alike, but one mind just thinks slightly faster than the other.

As we were paying for our meals, we heard a voice bellow from the far end of the alleyway.

"You should not have returned to Toyko, boy!" The man pulled out a samurai sword and held it in front of him. I quickly turned around to see another shadowed figure at the other end. He stood there with his hood down, rain dripping from him, while he held a sword by his side. He looked up and laughed, before saying, "Don't you know, Sensei? I AM Toyko." Then, with a roar, he launched himself into the air toward the other man. Our heads snapped back as the waiter finally returned to our table with the receipt. We left a reasonable tip and decided to head for the party. The night was still young, and we were chancing for a dancing.

We checked the address of the party on Google Maps and got a taxi there. We were unsure of what to expect; we had never been to a Japanese party before. We knocked on the door and a friendly lady answered the door.

"Welcome. You know, only one of you had to knock," she said with a laugh.

Paulie replied with, "I didn't realise we were knock, knock, knocking on heaven's door!" a line he had clearly prepared to say regardless of what she said. The woman crunched her eyebrows and said, "Right. Ehh, come on in."

Much to our dismay, there wasn't a single Japanese person at the party. It turns out the whole party was organised by an American guy who was living in Japan. He only seemed to invite Europeans and other Americans. He also seemed to be pushing a sort of Anti-Japanese rhetoric – claiming that he wishes he was alive in the mid-1940s. I avoided him for the night. Despite that, I saw what I believed to be the woman of my dreams – a woman that ticked all the boxes for me: she was shorter than me, she had an infectious smile, and she wasn't racist. Her eyes caught mine from across the room and then we both smiled. I shimmied and shook my way over to her. I looked her dead in the eyes, and I said,

"Hey."

She replied instantaneously with "Hey."

"How are you? I'm Vito by the way."

"I'm good. I'm Jennifer." What a gorgeous name.

"So, like…" I paused for effect. "Do you like movies? You know, like films?"

"Eh yeah I guess so," she said. She's a film buff just like me.

"Oh my God, I'm the same. That's so funny. I like them too." I laughed because of how well it was going, but also to comfort her. "Superhero."

"What?" she asked. No better way to keep a conversation going than by asking questions.

I laughed. "Sorry! I mean, like, I love superhero movies. You know like Marvel, DC. Spiderman is my favourite. I also like Thor. Who's your favourite?"

"Oh sorry, my friend is calling me. I should probably go." I have enough experience with the ladies to know when a girl is setting me up to ask for her number.

"Hey," I said. "Can I get your number?"

"Urm sure…" She quickly wrote down her number before heading over to her friends. I turned around and punched the air with glee. In the moment, I was pretty sure I had caught me a special one. But in the end, I never tried to call her because the more I thought about it the more I realised she wasn't really good looking enough for me. She was a nice girl all the same, but personality can only get you so far on the Vito Express.

I would consider my trip to Japan a success. On my journey I discovered games I'd never heard of, ate food I didn't know existed, and met a woman who was truly mediocre. I learned a lot about the culture of Japan, yet not too much that it bored me. Do I plan on revisiting? Yes. Of course I do. Asia is like a second home to me now. In the coming months I plan on visiting China to find out what those guys are up to. In the meantime, I will continue to eat my sushi at home and dream about the girl that gave me a fake number. I mean, the girl who I chose not to call, because I was the one who wasn't interested, because she wasn't as attractive as she thought she was.

Cairo

Location: Egypt
Population: Sorry, I forgot my abacus
Language Spoken: To me? English
Notable Inventions: Pyramids, Slavery, and Rivers (long ones)
Notable People: Tutankhamun, Niall, and Cleopatra

It was the first time I got to use my water jet pack for travel, rather than just using it for my YouTube videos. See now, the thing is, when the idea of a jet pack is brought up, we all think it's futuristic and we think of the likes of Boba Fett or Iron Man. I'll tell you what: It's all well and good until you're into your third hour on a seven-hour journey. It's not like you can just whip out your phone or read a great book like *Clownbound*. You need to focus 100% on your balance, winds, direction… THE WORKS! If you take your eye off the ball for a second, you're screwed. I would take a Ryanair flight instead a jetpack ride for any journey that takes over an hour.

I finally arrived at the beach with a rocky enough landing, and by that, I mean I hit several rocks while I was landing. It was to be expected really; I was as tired as that beach was sandy. My guide found me quite easily as I was the only one on the beach holding my knee in the air and had blood running down from my helmet and into my eyes. She helped me up and supported me as I limped off of the beach.

"Lovely to finally meet an Egyptian!" I said with joy seeing as this girl was the only person I got to talk to in nearly half a day.

"I'm only half Egyptian actually," she said with a giggle.

"Which half?"

"What?"

After I said this, I passed out from the excessive bleeding coming from my head.

I awoke in a shock. I was in some kind of luxurious hospital. There was a very small number of beds in there and, at most, a total of five medical staff working in there. It looked like millions were spent to build this hospital, but hey… It's better than spending billions on no hospital. It would be worse if that no hospital was for children too. Luckily, that kind of situation is unimaginable.

I felt nearly paralysed in my state. My initial fear was that there was something seriously wrong with me. I flicked my eyes to my bedside and there was my half Egyptian tour guide.

"Owen, you don't look so good. I've taken the liberty of booking you an early flight home. You are in no condition to see what Egypt has to offer."

I raised an eyebrow as if to say, 'what did you just say to me woman?' While looking at her, however, I caught a glimpse of my right arm. It was all bandaged up. I then flicked my eyes to the left; that arm was bandaged up too. My arms weren't sore though…

My tour guide left the room. I lay there upset, promising myself that I would never buy another jetpack for any reason again. Only planes from now on. Because I had been unconscious for so long, I couldn't sleep, and the night seemed to go on forever.

I got bored so I tried to wiggle my toes (without much luck), when all of a sudden, a grandfather clock sitting in the corner of the room erupted into a massive tune; song of the summer probably. The clock was loud, but the roars coming from around the room were louder. I was like a deer in headlights; I couldn't move and I feared for my life. My breathing got heavier and sweat was trickling down to my eyes. The roars got louder and louder, but then, as they got louder, they got jollier.

"MUMMIES!!!!" I screamed, finding my voice and gaining back my ability to move by covering my face with my bandaged-up arms. Following this little tissy I threw, a burst of laughter and giggles erupted all around me, as if the tickle monster had kidnapped several children and started doing what he does best to them in his tickle chamber. The room was now filled with bandaged-up broads.

"Well how did you end up here, stranger? Been a while since we had a new Mummy come in," one said.

"I ain't no Mummy. Heck, I ain't even a Daddy."

"You sure about that?"

One of the Mummies walked over to me as if she couldn't bend her legs. She went out to grab my belly, but I didn't feel anything. I looked down and saw that my entire body was wrapped up just like them. She took a loose end of the cloth that was wrapped around me and pulled. I was yanked into a quick spin but was stopped by her when I was facing a mirror. I nearly looked exactly like one of them, except my skin was still it's usual silky tan beneath the cloth. Was I one of them now?

"There is no need to be scared," one of them started. "It's not the end of the world."

Looking back at her in the mirror I said, "Well it's not ideal is it? Am I dead or what?"

"No, you're worse than dead…"

"Wha— What do you mean? What's worse than dead?"

"Well… You're apparently just the right amount of injured not to be shown a great tour around Egypt."

I punched the mirror in front of me as hard as I could, making it shatter into a thousand pieces.

"DON'T REMIND ME!" I was hysterical, ripping down paintings and throwing chairs. They all looked at me, knowing that they will never truly understand the pain I was going through because they had all already seen what Egypt has to offer. Once I was done trashing the room, I sat back down on the edge of my bed, panting from wrecking the room and unmaking the other Mummies' beds. The Mummies walked away, remade their beds, and then sat around a table to chat. A few minutes later, they returned to my bedside.

"Hey," said one of the Mummies with three other Mummies behind her, all of them looking as nervous as the next.

"What do you want…"

"Well, us Mummies got together and had a talk. We couldn't possibly know what you're going through right now…"

"BAH!" I yelled at them. "Spare me! If anything, you should just be talking about how great Egypt is and how I'll NEVER get to see it!"

"As a matter of fact, that did come up in our talk. Egypt is a fantastic place to behold. How would you like to see it?"

"Eh, obviously I'd love to, that's why I'm here you pile of toilet p-" I still can't believe it took me that long to realise that it wasn't a question, it was an offer.

It was already 1:30am and I had to be back here at 8am to get picked up for my flight. I joined the group around the table where they had already made out a schedule of where we would go, but it didn't make much sense. It said, for example, that I was going to spend some time below the River Nile. I had faith in them though, because if you can't trust your Mummy who can you trust. By 2am, we were out the door.

2am

I wasn't surprised to find out that the hospital was built inside one of the pyramids. The shape of the roof was a dead giveaway. What wasn't a dead giveaway was that the Mummies would be giving me a tour of this sandy land. I suppose, who would know it better than those who have lived here for thousands of years? They took me to see all of the other pyramids too, but I suppose once you've seen one, you've seen them all.

3am

They took me to see that musical 'Cats'. It was a disaster; the entire cast was filled with those Sphinx cats and they forgot all of their lines. They just wandered around the stage.

4am

Still at the show.

5am

Still at the damn show. I think the Mummies were enjoying it. HOW!?

6am

We were brought backstage to meet the cast and it was one of the worst experiences of my life, probably worse than the show. They insisted we pet them. The Mummies seemed to have no problem with this. It felt as though I was petting an old man's hanging neck flab. Hard to believe they're related to Simba.

"You generally have to be a young person to understand that show," mentioned one of the Mummies.

"Well, I didn't like it at all!"

"What are you senile?"

"No, I haven't seen the Nile yet. Hope I do while I'm here, though." I replied only half listening.

We got chased out after I took a whizz in one of their litter boxes. They were not happy about that at all.

7am

An hour to go and I was feeling as if I had not captured the essence of Egypt that I had dreamt of before this trip.

I wasn't expecting much for our final hour, but I was confident that it would be better than the show. One thing I noticed is that nobody else seemed to be out at night except Mummies; not just the Mummies I was hanging with, but several other Mummies I hadn't met. Several stores tend to be 24/7 and literally flip around to become a different store come midnight for Mummies. I would sum it up by saying Cairo has a great nightlife, but I can't really say that because the majority of them aren't *really* alive.

For my final location, the Mummies took me to the River Nile. The longest river in the world. It can be seen from space! But then again, I could potentially be seen from space, really depends on your eyesight. I had forgotten my swimming trunks, but even if I did have them, I wouldn't have been able to get in, what with the bandages and the sheer embarrassment of girls watching me try to swim.

"Do we get on a boat from here or what's the deal?" I asked, doing my best to avoid swimming at all costs.

"Kind of, but you're going to get into this to go where we want to show you."

To my dismay, they unfolded an adult size pram. I got in and it was surprisingly cozy!

The Mummies pushed me out in my neat little pram to the end of a dock in the river. There we waited for almost a minute for something to happen. I didn't mind if we waited there all day; the pram lifestyle was one I could get used to. Before my eyes, while I was tightly grasping the safety belt on the pram, an Egyptian godlike creature rose from the river. He was over 10 feet tall and wore some kind of dog mask… Might have been a kink for him or something.

"Whomst is the pram man?" The god echoed.

"Someone who has not experienced the city of Cairo to its fullest…"

A few tears ran down the god's chest from beneath his mask. He was audibly weeping. "LET HIM IN GOD DAMMIT!" he roared once more.

And just like that he stepped back down into the river. As quick as he went, the section of the dock began to lower. Thinking that I was going to drown, I quickly yanked down the pram's rain cover and hoped for the best. I closed my eyes and tried to think happy thoughts, such as someone telling I'm a pretty little boy. After a few seconds when I thought I was going to feel water, I chanced opening my eyes and witnessed impossible magic. There was some kind of force field surrounding us, protecting us from the water slipping in. It was as if we were in an elevator to god knows where. Literally, god knows where because I really do think that dog man was a god.

It took about thirty seconds for this magical elevator to come to a halt. When it did, I got the shock of my life to find out it was a nightclub.

"Ah! It's been many a moon since I've seen some fresh blood in this place!" welcomed a man with water for hair.

"Who are you and why are you leaning on my pram," I said while reclining my seat back a little further.

This question sent the Mummies into panic. A frenzy of apologies to the man/waterman for what I had said.

"Now now ladies! That's quite alright… Lil' man." He popped his collar, flicked his water hair back, splashing everyone behind him, and pointed at me with his hands shaped as guns while biting down on his lip. "I'm Niall."

He brought us to the back room and offered us all some water straight from his hair.

"Off my hair, a camel could survive a year in the desert. It has even been reported that the one that drank it grew another hump!" said Niall proudly.

"Didn't that turn out to be a tumour?" responded one of my Mummies.

"Pyramid, pieramid, what's the difference."

"Riiiight. So you own the Nile?" I asked, trying my best to get off of the topic of camel tumours, because I knew a camel that had a tumour back home at the time.

*****R.I.P. CAMELIA*****

"NO NO! It was just named after me. You really don't know much about your Egyptian history, do you?"

"Well, that's one of the main reasons why I came here actually. I'm something of a traveller."

"A traveller?!" shouted Niall, his hand now hovering dangerously close to a hammer.

"Yeah, I've travelled to many corners of the globe, discovering first-hand what this world has to offer!" I said as if I was defending myself in a court case.

"Oh, ok good," Niall said, now slowly bringing his hand away from the hammer.

"Can you tell me the history behind the Nile then? I don't have much time left here."

"I'd be delighted! Lie back in that pram there and I'll give you a little crash course. To begin, the river was a gift from me. The river was how long my hair used to be. People were starving, and I was in love..."

The story was crazy, with twists and turns you would not believe. I was getting really into it, until I started noticing the scenery around me.

I looked around and saw a theme, a familiar theme. Dishes filled with milk, bowls overflowing with fish-shaped treats, empty cardboard boxes filled with fur, and most notably… litter boxes in every corner of the room. I instinctively interrupted his story by yelling, "OH RATS! I'VE BEEN HAD! GET ME THE HELL OUT OF HERE!"

Sure enough, as soon as I did, the cats from the show barrelled into the room like there was a fish market. I braced myself in the seat and to the Mummies credit, we escaped safely, only losing the 'lives' of 3 Mummies in the great getaway. I heard they were unravelled like a ball of yarn.

8am

I got back to the hospital and it was as if nothing had happened. The grandfather clock erupted once again, and the Mummies were back laying still in their beds. I, however, was fully mobile. I wasn't there long enough to actually understand how this kind of voodoo magic worked. Maybe someday someone will explain it to me. My former tour guide got me on my plane in no time. On the plane, I looked out the window as it took off to bring me home. I saw a message written out in the sand saying, 'COME BACK SOON, OWEN!' I smiled to myself, thinking about how much I was welcomed there.

The dinner on the plane was handed out extremely early, while I was still looking out the window. A tray was placed in front of me. I looked down at it. '*What the hell?*' I thought and as quick as I had noticed a vacuum sealed, cheesy lasagne was placed in front of me, I realised there was a butcher knife pinned against my throat.

"You'll need something sharp to get that open," whispered the plane steward.

I put my hands up and looked to see who it was. Alas, it was one of the damn cats from the musical. I knew those scrawny cats could talk.

Moscow

Location: Soviet Union
Population: 11.9 Million
Language Spoken: Russian
Notable Inventions: Radio, Television, Medicine, and War and Peace
Notable People: Vladimir Putin, Vladimir Lenin, Ayn Rand, and Maria Sharapova

I ~~vas~~ was given opportunity to visit Moscow, Russia last year. I am American and I have never stepped foot on Russia before this. The Russian state newspaper ask me to write an article and I say, “Who me? An American?” and they say, “Yes, we want outside opinion!” I am definitely not Russian, so I say yes. However, might I say that Russia is best country in the world without the doubt! I loved it! As American, I want to say it was better than United States in almost every way.

I arrived at Sheremetyevo International Airport at the dawn and I was ready to see what Moscow had to offer. We drive straight to the Moscow Red Square. The taxi guy take me down ~~the M11 onto the ш. Ленинградское to Ленинградский пр-т. in Москва until we take the ул. 1-я Тверская-Ямская and ул. Тверская to ул. Ильинка~~ road. Next thing I know we are in Red Square. Very good roads. And wow. What a sight! I never see square like this in America! The Kremlin and Citadel looks most amazing. I saw a group of the homosexuals around the Red Square. I had conversation with them, and they told me how Russia treat them very well with no issue. I said, “But in my country they say you are treated bad by Russia!” and they said that the Americans lie about this. “No way dude,” I tell them. I couldn’t believe that my country would lie as such. However, they showed me proof of such and so now I know the America media is lying. I confirm that Russia treats gays very well!

After this I bumped into Putin. Wow! He was shaking everybody’s hands and giving food to poor children. He pointed at me and ask, “Are you American?” I say yes and he says, “It doesn’t matter. We love everybody here in Russia!” Wow. The orange guy never say this to me. I was lucky to be given look around the Russia military base. I was blown away by all of the many peace equipment and army machines! I work for US army and they have nothing compared to the Russia army. Putin then explains me how Russia never try to provoke other country and that America is the real enemy of the world. “What, dude,” I say. “Bro. You are crazy. My country is too awesome for this!” But he seemed so sure. So, I ask Putin, “What about Finland?” He tells me that Russia have no troops in the Finland and that Russia never tried to take the Finland. “What!” I say. “That’s crazy, dude! In my country we are always saying this about that!” And Putin then showed me proof of that they don’t have troops in the Finland. Incredible! Another United States lie! I then leave for the Red Square again. Thank you, Putin, for great time.

Suddenly it begins snowing! Wow, so cold. This is not like California sun that I am used to. Brrr. *Holy cow!* I thought to myself. Out of no place comes a man who says I can stay in his house. Wow, very nice. I go in and he offer me a glass of vodka. “I have never drank vodka before,” I say. “I only drink the Budweiser and the Coors!” I was worried because maybe this vodka not as good as American alcohol and I need to lie to the man! But after I drink it I say, “WOW. Now this is drink! Yum. Much better than American alcohol.” If my frat friends from my college heard me say this, they would be saying to me, “Bro, what the hell!” He then introduced me to his pet bear. He was big and strong and he showed me how to wrestle the bear. In America I won the four NCAA wrestling titles, so I am one of best America wrestlers. Yet, I cannot outwrestle bear! But the man then beats the bear very easily. The man explains me that Russians are better wrestlers than Americans and he show me proof of such! Wow. I did not know this.

The next day I go back to America and needless to say I was disappointed to be home. I really wish I could be Russian instead of American. How amazing this would be! If I had to rate my time in Moscow, I would give it 10 American style hot dogs out of 10! I look forward to going back to ~~my home~~ Moscow.

The Venice Boardwalk

Location: Los Angeles
Population: 40,000
Language: Italian (I think)
Notable Inventions: Roller blades, Pecs, and Stubbornness
Notable people: Chad, Stacy, and Brad

It was a time of need. A private plane was called to ensure my safety. A nine-hour flight with no sleep took its toll on me as the jetlag of a longer day battered my eyes. In the early hours of my journey I studied Italian to be able to interact with the locals. In the final hours of the journey, I researched how I should behave and places to avoid in the area - the areas where the battles were taking place.

The pilot left his cockpit to come and tell me that we were going to land in 20 minutes, and that I should now change into appropriate attire. After a brief nod, I went to the small bathroom at the back of the plane. There I opened my bag and pulled out a bedsheet, which I wrapped around myself like a toga.

The plane landed and a staircase rushed to meet it. I threw my backpack over my shoulder once more, filled with my ordinary clothes, a laptop and the first edition of *'Italian for Those Who Want to Learn Italian Without Paying a lot of Money, Relative to a Tutor, Say.'* I stood at the door of the plane gazing down at an empty pimped-out golf cart. In front of the cart stood three members of the Frat Senate who would take care of me on this expedition. They all looked just about the same. Toga worn across their bodies, same as me. They all sported black Oakley sunglasses, walked on black NIKE sliders and shared the same haircut of 'a one back and sides with a trim on top, please'.

"I welcome you to our land. Unfortunately, you come at a time of great peril, my bro," greeted a man who appeared to be in charge.

"A pleasure. There never seems to be a dull moment on the boardwalk," I replied.

After an exchange of fist bumping and hi-fives to secure peaceful intentions between us, the leader continued to announce, "Let us make haste. Time is of the essence and the backyard cookout will be gnarly if we arrive too late."

In the cart, I decided to ask the questions that I felt were hanging in the air, the unspoken truths. I felt they needed to be addressed sooner rather than later.

"What say you of the Battles of the Boardwalks?" I asked the room, a room without walls albeit.

"Common, I say. Ruthless and problematic," one of the other identical men muttered.

"No progress? No hope of an end?!" I whimpered with concern, which drew the cart back to a silence.

The journey took only ten minutes to get to the backyard cookout the boys had mentioned. Arriving outside the Frat house, a racket could be heard from inside the huge two-story wooden doors on the front of the enormous six story house. When we got out of the cart, everyone except myself and the driver headed out and around the mansion toward the backyard cookout. My instincts told me to join them. Then, I felt the driver's hand on my shoulder.

"For us, the time for joy and kegstands is not appropriate. Follow me at once."

He pulled up his toga sheet higher to avoid dirtying it against the rubbish left all across the front yard. It was covered in beer cans, the leftovers of Chinese takeaway boxes and other unspeakable things that would drive any environmentalist up the walls. Most of these things were half covered in single ply toilet paper too. Truly a mess. Typical of these boys, though.

It took me longer than my new friend to get to the Roman column supported porch, or the Fratio as they call it (similar to patio), as he knew where to step, whereas I felt I was stuck in a maze and could not find a clean patch to step on. At the front door he waited for me, holding it open as I stepped in. My eyes were met with a wondrously huge and glamourous room, the only other door in the building being the back door. It was a studio house that had been transformed to look like the inside of the Colosseum. There was a huge pit in the middle of the room about seven feet below the ground and a circle of steps surrounding it that rose as far as where I stood. The steps were filled with other bros wearing white togas around themselves. Some even had leaves in their hair or resting atop their ears. Few stood at a time to discuss a topic. The announcements were often met with an eruption of "OI OI OI!!!" in refusal or discontent. There was also an oddly strong smell of body odour and beer burps that made your nostrils want to shut up shop for the day.

As I sat on the steps, as high as I possibly could to avoid being part of the talks, things began to heat up quickly and get out of hand in the talks beneath us.

"My dudes, these fights have gone on too long. We all just gotta smoke up and enjoy the good times," said a man with dreadlocks to my left. Another man stood up.

"Bro, me and the boys got together last weekend at the kicker. We concluded dude, you smoke up too much!" This brought the Senate to its feet in rabbles. One man raced down the steps to the centre and shook his arms in the air to calm everyone down.

"CHILL, BROS! CHILL!" The noise trickled down into nothing in a few seconds. He then pointed to the accuser. "Bro! You just went against our pledge. DON'T… DISS… FELLOW… BROS! Don't make me swirly you for two hours straight again. I've never seen anyone want to go back to the hazing room, bro, but you might be a first!?"

The accuser let his head bow and reoccupied his seat. The man stayed beneath us and stood his ground.

The man was wearing an 'Under Armour' cap and flicked it backward on his head.

"Are we planning on spending the whole Summer here? Harshing each other? Don't burn each other, dudes… Burn your bi's and tri's in the gym! Burn out your tires at a kicker! Burn your lungs with a sticky one - BUT - never burn your bros!" He raised a can of beer he had hidden under his toga and kept it there for a few seconds. All around the senate, every member suddenly had a can raised above their heads too, including my friend beside me. Then, in sync, they all began to scream and hit the can off of their head to bust it open. They began to suck on the hole and open it from the top. I'd never seen anything like it.

I nudged my friend on the side. "What the hell was that?"

"It's called a shotgun, bro."

"You know you can drink it from the top, right?"

"You know you can shut the frick up, nerd, right?"

The bro down the centre of the room threw the can over his shoulder and into the near overflowing recycling bin, then wiped his mouth and continued.

"Men, let us get back to the war at hand before we go out back and get crunk. The guys on steroids have been fighting on the Venice Boardwalk for over two months now. We must discuss the war. The war of the innie/outties. A sombre topic, yes. Needs fixing? Absolutely. The world watches. What sayeth the nerd?"

The man cleared the stage, to let the floor disappear. Arose a cage through the floor and in it, some nerd.

"Got an answer for us yet, Einstein?" asked a sarcastic Senator.

"Not yet, guys. It's really hard and you guys haven't been feeding me very mu-"

"Back in the hole!" yelled the crowd together and the cage began to sink once more.

"The battles of the innie and outtie belly buttons continue as we sit here. Innocents die and the warriors grow stronger from all the 'roids they inject in their bums. We need a solution and this Senate does not seem to have it," I said with fury under my breath.

"Well then poindexter's laboratory, where's your answer?"

Embarrassed not to have one, I excused myself to the bathroom even though I didn't even really need to go. It was based outside. When I got there, it was clogged. "Typical," I moaned. I got a plunger to fix it. Then before I even started going to work on it, I got an idea.

I sprinted down the steps with the plunger in my hand, my footsteps echoing through the silent room, catching the attention of everyone. My friend chased me and called after me, but I ignored his calls. I stood at the bottom and tried to speak in a language where they might understand me. I held the plunger up and this is what I said:

"Bros, I don't think you know me. My friends call me Jackson Five, though, because I'm as easy-going as ABC and I hooked up with Janet Jackson this one time." I looked at the man who was in the pit just before me for approval.

"Frat-tastic," he said. So, I continued.

"My dudes, I know how to get us out of this sticky mess, aight? It's gonna be lit!"

People began to whisper. Whispers got so loud that I couldn't even share my idea. Luckily, it all calmed down in a few seconds.

"I need two volunteers."

Two identical men from the front stood up and came to me.

"Remove the top half of your robes."

They shared a look of concern. Then, just as I had, they looked up to the man previously in the pit for approval. He nodded. They untied the knot on their shoulder and looked at me through their black Oakleys.

"Everyone, these two brothers are identical. However, by chance, one has an innie and the other an outtie. The reasoning behind the war. Now look at this."

I walked over to the man with an innie bellybutton, put the end of the plunger on the bellybutton, pressed, then pulled. He now had an outtie bellybutton. The brothers were now the same in the eyes of the 'roid boys on the Venice Boardwalk.

The Senate was stunned. Before a slow clap began, Juuls could be heard hitting the floor. The answer had just appeared in front of their very eyes.

“There is still one problem at hand: we gotta distract the innies if we’re going to get a chance to get this plunger on their raging abs. Going near them without a distraction is a suicide mission.”

“We got a distraction, man,” said a fellow Senator. He then flexed his bicep.

“You think they’ll look at that? These guys are monsters,” I replied shaking my head.

“Not my guns, you nimrod!”

I then noticed he was actually pointing upward.

I tilted my head up, not realizing just how high the ceiling travelled and up there was another cage - a cage with a woman inside. She had bleach blonde hair, fake tan covering her entire body and enough jewellery to make a Pharaoh say, “You’re overdoing it a bit there.” She must have been extremely cold too because all she wore besides the jewellery was a sports bra, black Adidas short shorts and red high heels.

“You just keep a girl locked up there by herself, day in day out? That’s inhumane…” I said.

“You’d think so, but she won’t leave the house. She keeps trying to score with every guy here, but it gets annoying after a while, so we keep her up there, bro. No biggie,” said a different member of the senate sitting on the fourth step up.

I made way for the cage to be lowered to the pit. The cage remained shut and everyone present on the lower tier of the steps got up and cleared for a safe distance. The girl began shouting.

“Hey boys! Guess who’s single!” she screamed.

The leader interjected with a louder scream, “Do not be tempted boys. For those who go near the ‘Frat Rat’ will leave this Fraternity and never return.”

“My guy friends say I’m just like one of the boys, haha! I play video games and drink beers with them!” she continued to yell desperately while the room either looked away or shook their heads at her.

“Why is she called a ‘Frat Rat’?” I nudged to the person sitting beside me on the step I just retreated to.

"Rats are rodents. Hard to get rid of, are not wanted, and overstay their welcome. That's what she is," he said before spitting out some of his chewing tobacco into a jar.

The leader went down to the cage and stood beside it at a distance.

"The plan is evident. We will release the Frat Rat at noon, when the innie 'roid boys are at the protein shack, 'Swoley Poley's'. There she will start mirin' the roid boys. They will be distracted and that's when we will sneak up on them and plunger those jocks!"

The room roared and then shotgunned their beers. This time, I joined them.

We got to the boardwalk, incognito, wearing an inflatable muscle suit. We blended in perfectly because there were two hundred of us stuffed into one suit, perfectly replicating how big these guys were. It was as if we were just one 'roid boy out for his hourly shake. We were outside Swoley's where they all were - it was a protein shack as big as a Walmart, filled to the brim with muscle. There we gave the signal for the Frat Rat to be released from her cage. This had to be done remotely at a distance, as it wouldn't have been safe to go close to her. Once released from her cage, she let out her infectious roars.

"I'm like nearly Instagram famous. You should follow me!" She then pulled out a picture of a starving African child from her back pocket and held it above her for all to see. "Me, when no one will take me to go get some chicken nuggets!"

These outbursts caused the innie 'roid boys that were swarming the shack to turn their heads with curiosity, like they were someone coming home from work, trying to see the amount of damage done to a car crash that they were driving by on the motorway even though it's none of their damn business.

Sure enough, the 'roid boys' attention was captivated. That's when we made our move, taking a plunger out of the body suit we were all wearing. We gradually wedged our way through the crowd, getting to everyone slowly but surely. They were all hypnotized like the Frat Rat was Medusa and she had them under her annoying spell. The 'roid boys loved the attention, the attention they'd desired ever since they started lifting weights and started injected 'roids into their bums.

The plunger was practically silent in comparison to how loud the Frat Rat was. It took hours, but we eventually got all of them. We returned to the mansion and partied for a full week. Just the boys. I came out of the house looking just like one of them. Toga still on, NIKE sliders, Oakley sunglasses and a 'one back and sides with a trim on top, please' haircut. It would take a while for the war to come to a complete halt, but that day I tried my arm. I went to the Venice Boardwalk by myself.

The ruins were gone, the dents in the walls and wooden flooring were no more. There were shops open, there were people that weren't 30 feet tall wandering around, socializing and minding their own business. It was 25 degrees Celsius. Not a cloud in the sky. Laughter and joy in the air. On my walk, I even chanced my arm even further and walked by the outdoor beach gym to investigate any fights or mayhem, just to see if there was still hate on the Venice Boardwalk, but no. All the 'roid boys were now at peace. The war was over, and the battles had ceased. The Venice Boardwalk was once again a beautiful location with lovely people. I went to the churro stand and got myself one, crossed the way after waiting for a dozen people on rollerblades to skate by. I looked over the wooden railing, where I could see the sunset and the length of the boardwalk all at once. It was a new Venice Boardwalk I was looking at, a place of wonder and hope for the future. It was the first time I got to see her like this. I bit into my cinnamon sweet churro and after I swallowed, I said to her, "Bonjourno."

Sydney

Location: Australia
Population: 4.6 million
Language Spoken: Australian
Notable Inventions: Spiders, The Great Barrier Reef, and Home & Away
Notable People: Steve Irwin, Jason Blade, and Kangaroo Jack

G'day mate! My name is Rachel, and today I'll be telling you all about my recent trip to the land down under: Sydney, Australia. A place known for its beauty, wildlife, and unruly desire to kill you in every possible way. Did you know, Australia is home to 100 venomous snake species? Better pack that antivenom! But, of course, the snakes are only one thing to be worried about. You've also got the spiders, jellyfish, crocodiles and sharks to worry about. Isn't that just exciting? To be prepared I made sure to pack a full set of body armour that I was planning on wearing at all times. I knew the weather would be much hotter than what I'm used to, especially wearing full body armour, so I very wisely decided to go in early December when it wouldn't be as hot.

After a (thankfully) snake-free plane journey, we finally touched down in Australia. Once I had finished putting on my 3-inch thick vest, military helmet and steel-toed boots, I departed the plane. To my surprise, I did not step out to a snowy winter wonderland, but rather a blazing sun and phenomenal heat. *This place must be hot all the damn time!* I thought. *I can only imagine what it's like in the summer!* Once I grabbed my bags, I began my arduous journey to the hotel. I walked beneath the beating sun, fighting off the local wildlife and only narrowly escaping with my life. The last thing I remember I was lying in the sand dying of dehydration, losing hope by the second. Just as I was about to lose consciousness, I saw the shimmering lights of my hotel in the distance and mustered enough strength to make it through the doors. I was a shell of my former self, covered in sand and drenched head to toe in sweat. The 10-minute journey from the airport was far worse than I was expecting.

Once I had finished frantically searching my room for spiders, I decided to venture out into the city. I noticed all the locals wearing shorts and T-shirts, so I came to the conclusion that all the deadly animals were asleep at this time of day and my body armour would not be necessary. I took a taxi to the biggest tourist attraction of Sydney, the Opera House. I asked one of the locals if he could show me where it was, and he pointed past me to a rather odd-looking building.

"Well crikey, Sheila, it's that beauty over there!"

"My name's Rachel actually and where?"

"Right there! Are ya blind, mate?"

"What, the hedgehog building?"

"Eh, come again, Sheila?"

"Rachel! That just looks like a hedgehog lying down. What's the deal with that?"

"You right mate? You haven't seen the Opera House before? It's actually a marvel of modern architecture! It was designed by Jorn Utzon in the late 20th century and has since become a staple of our city. It stands as one of the greatest pieces of architecture of the last century."

"You seem very proud of a building that looks like a dumb hedgehog."

After an extremely long conversation where I tried to convince him that the so-called "building" is ugly and everyone in the country should be ashamed of it, the man eventually gave me a rather defeated "Piss off," and walked away. *They're so rude here*, I thought to myself. I felt deflated after this exchange, or maybe it was because of the snake that had climbed itself into my boot. Either way I decided to relax by taking a trip to the beach.

The beach was packed full of people. There were people talking all sorts of nonsense about 'tinnies' and 'barbies'. The slang in Australia was something I just couldn't get the hang of. A man asked me if I had a 'ciggy', and then asked if I'd watched the 'footy.' What? Why can't they just speak American like normal people. I went for a swim in the sea to calm myself down from the frustration of how much I hated these people, but I ended up getting stung by 4 types of jellyfish instead. A man kindly offered to urinate on me to alleviate the pain, something clearly not uncommon around these parts. If I'm being honest, I thought it was quite nice of him and I have to say, I didn't find myself hating them as much from that point on. Let's just say there's plenty of land down under, if you catch my meaning.

I saw a man offering a shark cage dive on the beach.

"Oh my gosh! You'd let people get attacked by sharks? Isn't it dangerous?"

"It's perfectly safe, Sheila!"

"It's Rachel actually and umm no, of course it's dangerous. They're sharks!"

"Well actually, what you might not realise is that only around 6 humans are killed by sharks every year, and they're usually people that don't take proper precautions when approaching them. By comparison, humans kill at least 100 million sharks every year. That's an absolutely debilitating number and if it continues at this rate, it's likely to have an irreversible impact on life in the ocean. Sharks are at the top of the food chain in the world's oceans and they keep the numbers of other marine animals in check, so if they go extinct, everything will tip out of balance which is likely to lead to mass extinctions of other marine species. Sharks are wonderful creatures that have a rich diversity and unprecedented strength and agility, but they have no way of fighting back against our fishing trawlers. They're killed on a mass scale mostly just to make shark fin soup, which is a delicacy food in some parts of the world. In some cases, fishermen cut off all their fins and chuck them back into the ocean where they're left to die on the seafloor, completely helpless. So, you see, I think it's fair to say sharks aren't the evil ones; we are."

"Yeah, but like, have you seen *Jaws*? That thing is clearly pretty evil."

A conversation very similar to the one with Hedgehog House guy followed which left a bitter taste in my mouth and a surprising urge to kill sharks. I left the beach and started making my way to the next tourist stop on my list, the Australian Outback. Before that, however, I went to a restaurant to try the local cuisine of barbecued shrimp and a pint of what I can only describe as literal urine. For copyright reasons I won't name the brand of beer but let's just say it sounds a bit like "Fospers." I couldn't bring myself to eat fish because it just reminded me of the flesh-eating piranha that was still hanging out of my arm from the beach, so I sent it back and ordered a plate of lasagna instead. After paying for my delicious meal, I asked the waitress where I'd have to go to get to the Outback. She looked a little confused but then replied, "You can head out back through there, Sheila." She then pointed to a door on the other side of the restaurant.

"My name is Rachel!"

"Fair dinkum."

"I'm sure your income is very fair; thanks for telling me." *Weirdo*. "So, it's just through here, is it?"

"Aye, mate."

I walked towards the doors on the other side of the restaurant and made my way to the Australian Outback. I was absolutely shocked. On the other side of the door there were dumpsters filled to the brim with garbage and I even saw a rat running around. It looked just like any other alleyway in L.A. There were drawings on the walls ahead of me. *Those must be the Aboriginal cave paintings I've heard so much about!* I concluded. It was mostly just big green letters spelling phrases I couldn't understand. Some kind of ancient language, no doubt. I saw a tanned man with a black bushy beard smoking a cigarette across from me. An authentic Aboriginal man?! I couldn't miss my chance to learn all about his rich culture.

"EX-CUSE ME, SIR! I'M FROM A-MER-I-CA! DO YOU SPEAK A-MER-I-CAN?"

He gave me a confused look and responded in perfect American (but with a strong Australian accent):

"I'm from India actually."

It reminded me of back home the way Native Americans like to be called Indians. I accepted that this must just be a thing with native cultures.

"Oh, I understand! What can you tell me about your people?"

"My people? Excuse me?"

"The Aborig- I mean - *Indians*," I said with a wink.

"Listen, Sheila, I've gotta get back to work."

Feeling pretty peeved off, I left the outback and made my way back to the hotel. I had almost completed my list of goals for Australia, and my trip was mostly coming to an end. The only other thing on my list was to see a kangaroo. Unfortunately, the next morning I was rushed to hospital after 6 near-fatal spider bites that I got in my sleep, and I was kept there for the remainder of my vacation. I knew I should've worn my body armour to bed. Because of this, I never got to see that kangaroo. I wasn't too mad about it though, because I'm not an idiot and I'm aware that it's just a dude in a suit. There's no way any animal looks that weird.

Overall, I'd say Australia was an interesting experience. Despite the fact that I nearly died at least 6 times, and everyone kept getting my name wrong, I had a good time. It's interesting to experience other countries. I'm on the cusp of Sagittarius and Capricorn so obviously my Sagittarius side understands that the key to a fulfilling life is becoming aware of as many different cultures as possible. On the other hand, my Capricorn side loves being pissed on.

London

Location: England
Population: 8.1 Million
Language Spoken: English
Notable Inventions: Tea, Protestantism, and Colonialism
Notable People: The Queen, Cromwell, and Some Actors from Game of Thrones

Pip pip, well what's all this then? Are you muggin' me off? Hi, my name's Greg and today I'm going to be telling you all about the wonderful city of London! The home of the wide-reaching United Kingdom, right here in wonderful England. What can I say about this place? Everyone cycles around on penny farthings, wearing monocles and top hats. It's absolutely idyllic, my old chum. As a bonus, everyone is so kind and full of that good ol' English politeness. Not like the horrific warzone that is Dublin across the Irish sea, where those barbarians eat potatoes and pipe bomb each other every day while singing "I'm a Stupid Mick". You won't find anything like that here. The only acid on my face is the vinegar from my fish and chips! I would know because I have been to London many times. I'm there now actually. I'm looking at Large Benjamin right now. "Bing Bong," he tells me.

On my first trip to London I was just stunned by the scenery. The first thing that stands out is the enormous London Eye. I don't know why there's a massive eyeball in the middle of the city or who owns it. I don't know why they would want to watch me. Just that classic English quirkiness of course! I'm not scared of it. In no way has the thought of a huge eyeball staring at me ever stopped me from going to London out of debilitating fear. I told you, I've been there loads. I mean - here.

My next trip was to Buckingham castle to meet the Queen. She actually formally requested to meet me when she heard I was writing this travel guide. I walked into the throne room and waited for her to come in. The room was dimly lit, and everything was covered in gold. Before she came in, a suspicious looking man wearing all black approached me with a weird smile on his face. He came right up to me and whispered in my ear (which I thought was extremely odd) about how I should kneel when the Queen entered. "I have a reputation to maintain," he said in a peculiar accent that was impossible to define. Before long, the Queen herself entered the room and sat on the throne. She looked up at me and said, "You insolent fool, you were supposed to kneel!" to which I responded "Frankly, Mrs. Queenie, I couldn't give a Barney! You can take a good look at me own crown jewels, if you catch me meanin'!"

The Queen was so shocked that she fainted dramatically in her throne. I was promptly escorted to the tower of London where I was kept and to be tried for treason against the throne. For three days I sat in my jail cell, devising a plot to buy an Anonymous mask and overthrow the British government with bombs. Before I executed my plan however, I had a visitor. It was the Queen herself!

"Well, well, my boy I must say, you did *indeed* shock me so! However, I cannot deny you have serious moxey. Perhaps it should be you sitting on the throne and not I!" The man in black, once again, came startlingly close to me and whispered, "Distrusting me was the wisest thing you've done since you arrived in London," in that ever-elusive accent.

With that, I was back out on the streets of London ready to explore. For my next and final tourist destination I was to visit the leader of West London: West Minister Abbey. I made my way to 10 Downton Street and met with the woman over crumpets with another important political figure, the Earl of Gray. Together we discussed such extremely fun and exciting topics as Brexit and taxes. After hours of intense discussion and thrilling debates we came to the final conclusion: "Brexit means Brexit." The three of us will be accepting the Nobel Peace Prize for this discovery.

I joined them in the bar to celebrate our momentous achievement where we happened across a man in a tuxedo who appeared to be staring dramatically out the window, as though he had just experienced some personal crisis but was now devising a plan to overcome the seemingly insurmountable task ahead of him. He was drinking martinis by the bucketload and resisting the seductive nature of several attractive women. I asked him what his name was, and while I can't recall what it was, I do remember him saying his last name first, and then his first name, and then his last name again. After getting a message in his earpiece, he pressed a secret button on his Rolex and jetpacked through the ceiling. I watched him pull out a pistol in the air and shoot three flying terrorists in the head before landing in a fancy sports car and launching away. Bit of a oddball.

Later on in the evening I went for dinner in a classic London pub. I ordered the English staple of fish and chips, which I have to say, was quite the treat! Having tasted potatoes so fresh and so deliciously fluffy, I completely understand why the British would want to invade and massacre the Irish people for good farming land. I decided I'd enjoy a nice pint of lager after my dinner. This seems to be something of an English tradition, so I figured why not? I enjoyed it very much - a little too much I might add! One drink led to another, and another after that… Before long I was outside on the street surrounded by a group of young men, all of us shirtless, screaming at the top of our lungs, "COME ON YOU SLAGS!" at a group of young girls passing by. The rest of the night I don't remember very well but I know for sure that I ended up pulling a really attractive English girl. It was the girl from Countdown actually. She's my wife now.

Well, that just about wraps up my little adventure in the city of London, and what an adventure it was. If you're considering going there but you're not sure, just watch BBC series such as *Doctor Who* and *Sherlock* because the impression you get of the city and the people in it from watching those types of shows is completely accurate in every way. It's a wonderfully clean city that's full of posh and polite people. Not like it is in the disgusting hellscape that is Dublin. Never go there. It's not safe.

Bonus: Legoland

Location: Bermuda Triangle
Population: 0
Language Spoken: Hard to say
Notable Inventions: The Lego Block, a solid and efficient cement alternative
Notable People: Harry Potter (in Lego), All of the Ghostbusters (in Lego), Yoda (in Lego), and Legolas

Packing for this trip was harder than you think. I had 2 bags packed and was all set to go. I was about to walk out of the front door when I suddenly realised that they don't use cement mix in Legoland. *'I just saved myself 20 euro for baggage claim,'* I thought.

Going to Legoland is expensive (everyone knows that), but for no one to be on the plane to go there was a bit extreme. The plane was very old fashioned with the propellers on each wing slightly rusted, making a loud creaking sound as it moved. This made me worry if I was ever going to make it to this place of apparent wonder and cheer.

The plane barely took up off of the ground. Not even my heavy BEATS headphones could cancel the sound of metal on metal grinding in the plane's mechanics. Not even when I turned "Lil Wayne's Essentials' Spotify playlist full volume could I avoid the panicking screams inside my head. Not even Lil Wayne's repeating dance moves on my phone could distract me from the danger I was in.

The pilot left the cockpit to tell me to put on my safety belt. The plane was so small that there was no intercom. We hit turbulence HARD. The plane shook like it was a rattle in Michael J. Fox's hand. Concern over my safety led to more panic, panic led to fear, fear led to anger, anger led to the hate, hate led to dark sid… The plane felt as though it was giving up, even dying. Had it seen its final flight? Had I? Just like that, a piece of the plane ripped off on the opposite side, bringing with it 2 of the 14 passenger seats. I felt my body being sucked toward the hole. Clenching both of my armrests I closed my eyes and began to think if Legoland was really going to be worth this?

A dark thunderous cloud beckoned, and we were headed straight for it. I couldn't catch my breath to scream at the pilot to turn this damn plane around. Before I knew it, the plane was in the dark cloud and the room slowly filled with the black moisture that surrounded us. Everything went black. I was certain I was dead as everything seemed to stop. My legs stopped flailing. I could suddenly catch my breath and Lil Wayne was now the only sound I could hear. However, everything was still black around me. The black cloud began to clear and my vision was restored, although looking around me I still believed I was dead.

The whole plane was made of LEGO. The stewardess rose from her seat with a bag comparable to the size of Santa's sack of presents. She knelt down beside the side of the plane with a huge hole in it and began to rebuild it with the pieces of LEGO that filled the bag. It didn't take her long to finish fixing the wall. When she was finished, she stood up, brushed off the dust from her knees and said with a welcoming smile, "Welcome to Legoland, sir!"

I looked outside of the plane and looked on in wonder toward the island of LEGO that lay below me. It was small, but packed with skyscrapers, vehicles and people. It seemed like a perfectly functional city! We landed at the airport and there before me in arrivals was the Mayor of Legoland, my guide for my short time there.

"Hello there Sean, m'boy!" he bellowed.

"Pleasure to meet you mister Mayor!" I said nervously.

"Tell me Sean! Did you bring any cement mix?" now leaning in to me with curiosity and a faint smirk.

"I was going to but then I thou-"

"WELL YOU WON'T NEED ANY HERE!" he said, completely cutting me off with excitement.

From the airport, the Mayor had organised our own personal chauffeur, Jeff.

"You must be exhausted Sean! Jeff, drop Sean off at his Hotel and let him get settled in."

"Thank you so much mister Mayor."

"Please, please!" the Mayor waved back at me. "Call me 'The Official Mayor of Legoland.'"

In my penthouse hotel room, I realised that I had brought the wrong bag. I now had no spare clothes and 20kg of cement mix.

An hour later, I got a call from reception saying a ride was waiting for me outside. I was tempted to slide down the banister. Fortunately, as I was about to jump on, I saw all of the tiny LEGO pieces sticking out and realised I'd probably get a haemorrhoid if I even tried that. I raced down the stairs and greeted my tour guide again. He was eager to get started and show off the LEGO culture that this land had to offer.

He took me into the city, put his arm around my shoulder and began pointing around him.

"See there!? That's the LEGO Empire State Building! And over there, that's the LEGO Eiffel Tower!" With each new building he chuckled with excitement.

"Say, do you have any original LEGO culture? If you understand?"

"Oh, you mean you want to see some art! No problem at all!"

Just like that, he told Jeff to turn the car around. Within a few minutes we were at the LEGO Louvre. As soon as we got there, I came to the conclusion that he didn't understand what I meant by original culture.

"See, Sean! Over here we gots the LEGO *Mona Lisa* and over here the LEGO *Saint John the Baptist*! Lots of art in Legoland! OH YES!" bellowed the Mayor once more.

"Sir! Listen to me, Legoland seems to have no original entity to its land. No culture. Nothing unique! It seems that I am in a fraudulent land that has copied the best parts of every other country in the world. Why should I tell my readers to come here? It's a cheap knockoff of a destination."

"Sean, you are tired. Go back to the hotel and rest," the mayor said in a calming demeanour.

"I might be tired Sir, but I am right, and my mind won't be changed."

The Mayor continued with a sinister tone, "Jeff, make sure he gets back to his room at once."

I jumped into the backseat of the car, frustrated with the disappointment of Legoland. As I was putting on my seatbelt, the Mayor knocked on my window and gestured me to roll it down. He leaned his head into the window, so much so that I could easily smell the faint scent of coffee on his breath. Crumbs were easily noticeable on his beard too, possibly from some toast or a panini.

"You address me as 'The Official Mayor of Legoland', you ungrateful swine."

With that, he slapped the roof of the car and Jeff sped off. This ride back to the room seemed to take forever. There was a peculiar tension that even a goth, who claims they feel nothing, would be able to feel.

I fell asleep within about ten minutes. Maybe I was more tired than I thought, but as quick as I was coming into Legoland, I was leaving it. I awoke on a barge surrounded by piles of fish and a few fishermen. My suitcase was handcuffed to my hand, with a note taped to it. It read:

Sean,

I hurt that you could not find the culture that we see in Legoland, I really do. It is a pity you are forever forbidden from ever returning. You will be needing this cement mix where you are going. Which is NOT Legoland.

Regards, The Official Mayor of Legoland.

To summarise, Legoland has nothing new but their citizens are a proud people that refuse criticism. You should go if you only like LEGO and nothing else.

Conclusion

Well, your journey has finally come to an end. Let's reflect. Remember Rome? That was good, wasn't it? And Cairo! Don't get me started. And what about New York? Yeah!

But we bet your homesick from all that travelling. If you liked this book, make sure to join our newsletter at www.rwpublishing.net and check out *Clownbound: Take Me to the Circuits* on Amazon.

Also, if you liked this book don't be afraid to give us a review. Reviews help us a lot. Thank you for reading. We really appreciate your support!

Free eBook

Sign up to our newsletter at www.rwpublishing.net/newsletter and get the second book of the series absolutely free!

Printed in Great Britain
by Amazon

34183565R00047